ANATOLE

Also by Eve Titus with pictures by Paul Galdone
Anatole and the Cat
Anatole and the Piano
Anatole and the Thirty Thieves
Anatole Over Paris
Anatole and the Toy Shop

ANAT

OLE

by Eve Titus
Pictures by Paul Galdone

A BANTAM LITTLE ROOSTER BOOK
NEW YORK · TORONTO · LONDON · SYDNEY · AUCKLAND

For my son Richard

ANATOLE
*A Bantam Little Rooster Book / published by arrangement with
the author and illustrator's estate*

PRINTING HISTORY
McGraw-Hill edition published in 1956
*Special thanks to the Kerlan Collection at the University of Minnesota for
making original illustration materials available to us.*
*Little Rooster is a trademark of Bantam Books, a division of Bantam
Doubleday Dell Publishing Group, Inc.*
Bantam edition/July 1990

Library of Congress Cataloging-in-Publication Data
Titus, Eve.
    Anatole / by Eve Titus; illustrated by Paul Galdone. —Bantam
ed.
    p. cm.
    "A Bantam little rooster book."
    Summary: A French mouse decides to earn an honest living by
tasting the cheese in a cheese factory and leaving notes about its
quality.
    ISBN 0-553-34870-1
    [1. Mice—Fiction. 2. Cheese—Fiction.] I. Galdone, Paul, ill.
II. Title.
PZ7.T543A1 1990
[E]—dc20
                                                89-17591
                                                 CIP
                                                   AC

Published simultaneously in the United States and Canada

Bantam Books are published by Bantam Books, a division of Bantam
Doubleday Dell Publishing Group, Inc. Its trademark, consisting of
the words "Bantam Books" and the portrayal of a rooster, is Registered
in U.S. Patent and Trademark Office and in other countries. Marca
Registrada. Bantam Books, 666 Fifth Avenue, New York, New York
10103.

PRINTED IN THE UNITED STATES OF AMERICA

0 9 8 7 6 5 4 3 2

In all France
there was no happier, more contented mouse
than Anatole.

He lived in a small mouse village

near Paris

with his dear wife DOUCETTE

and their six charming children—

PAUL and PAULETTE

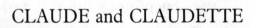

CLAUDE and CLAUDETTE

GEORGES and GEORGETTE.

Every evening as the sky darkened
the husbands and fathers bicycled along the boulevard toward Paris
to find food for their families.

Once arrived, they entered people's houses
through secret passageways, known only to themselves.
Anatole's partner was usually Gaston.

One night,
while they were looking for leftovers in someone's kitchen,
Anatole heard people in the next room talking about mice.
Curious, he crept under the sofa and listened.

"Oh, those terrible mice!" complained a woman.
"They sneak into my kitchen,
they rummage around in my garbage pail,
or pull themselves up to the table and take what is there.
Sometimes they even nibble at untasted food!
This I must throw away—
heaven knows how dirty their paws are!"

"They are a disgrace to all France," said a man angrily.
"To be a mouse is to be a villain!"

Deeply shocked, Anatole ran back to the kitchen.
"Gaston—we must leave at once!"

On the way home, Anatole, greatly upset,
told his friend what had happened.

"BAH! A mere trifle," scoffed Gaston.
"People are people, and mice are mice.
Our loved ones must eat,
and our only hunting-grounds are people's homes."

"But I never dreamed they regarded us this way,"
cried the unhappy Anatole.
"It is horrible to feel scorned and unwanted!
Where is my self-respect? My pride? MY HONOR?"

Gaston shrugged his shoulders indifferently.
"Resign yourself, Anatole. *C'est la vie!*"

Doucette comforted him.
"You are so right, Anatole," she said sadly.
"If only we could give people something in return—
but alas, that is impossible!"

Anatole jumped up and danced Doucette around the room.
"Impossible? Perhaps not, *ma petite*!
You have given me a wonderful idea."

16

He sat down at the typewriter
and typed thirty or forty signs that said:

```
EXTRA-'SPECIALLY GOOD
             'SPECIALLY GOOD
                     GOOD
                        NOT SO GOOD
                              NO GOOD
```

Then he stuck a long pin through each sign
and put them all away carefully in his briefcase.

Riding to Paris that evening, Anatole said,
"Gaston, will you feel insulted if I go off alone after this?
I have an idea that I must work on in secret."

Gaston answered, "I am your friend, *n'est-ce-pas*?
A friend is never insulted—a friend has faith. Good luck!"

When they reached Paris, Anatole left the others
and headed toward the business part of town.
He parked his bicycle in front of the Duval Cheese Factory.

He squeezed his small mouse's body easily under the door,
not forgetting his briefcase.
How heavenly it smelled inside!
His sensitive nose sniffed many delicious cheeses—
CAMEMBERT, PORT SALUT, BLEU, ST. MARCELIN, ROQUEFORT, BRIE.

Well, thought Anatole—I mustn't stand here sniffing all night.
There is work to be done!

He hurried down one dark passageway after another
until he found what he was looking for—
the Cheese-Tasting Room!

It was dimly lit, filled with long, wooden tables.
On them stood great mounds of cheese, of all shapes and sizes.

Without further delay, Anatole climbed up on the nearest table.
First he tasted a bit of Camembert.
"Mmm! Couldn't be better!"
He opened his briefcase, took out an EXTRA-'SPECIALLY GOOD sign,
and pinned it on the cheese.

The next one tasted much too sharp.
He used a NOT SO GOOD sign, and wrote something on it in pencil.

Up and down the long rows of cheeses went Anatole,
for hours and hours,
sniffing and tasting and pinning on signs.

At last his work was finished.

"*Voilà!* Now the Duval Factory will learn a thing or two.
Mice are known everywhere as the World's Best Judges of Cheese!
And as for myself, I shall bring some home proudly,
for I have honorably earned it!"

Next morning at the factory there was great excitement.
Everyone wondered who had written the strange little signs.
In marched M'sieu Duval himself.
"We'll soon see just how much this Anatole knows about cheese!"
He tasted some Roquefort.
"*Touché!* Anatole is right—this *does* need more orange peel!
Now listen, all of you—business has been none too good lately.
We'll try making cheese Anatole's way,
and see what happens."

Every night Anatole left more of his little signs.
And every day the cheese workers made more changes.

Soon business began to BOOM!
The people of France demanded Duval cheese or no cheese at all!
Orders poured in so fast that M'sieu Duval enlarged his factory
and gave everybody a raise in salary.

But he couldn't discover who was leaving the signs.

"Why doesn't Anatole appear?" M'sieu Duval asked his secretary.
"He deserves to be rewarded—
we owe all our good fortune to him!"

He wrote a little note, begging to meet Anatole.
But Anatole wrote back that he preferred to remain unknown.

M'sieu Duval even had every employee named Anatole
come to his office for questioning.
But each one denied that he had left the signs.

It was no use—the secret remained a secret!

Then one afternoon M'sieu Duval rang for his secretary,
and dictated a very long letter.

That night Anatole found the letter.

DUVAL
LE MEILLEUR FROMAGE DU MONDE

My Dear Anatole,

This letter comes to thank you for all you have done. Our success is due entirely to your wonderful work!

I am most eager to meet you in person, but since you prefer to remain unknown, I shall respect your secret.

Whoever you are, it is clear that you love cheese greatly. Please help yourself to all the cheese you like, as often as you like. Every night there will be some good French bread left here for you, and chocolate éclairs, and other dainties. How I wish I could reward you more richly!

Anatole — We Salute You! From now on we shall think of you fondly as

FIRST VICE-PRESIDENT
IN CHARGE OF CHEESE-TASTING!

Remember — you are <u>always</u> welcome here!

With every good wish for your happiness,

Your friend,

Henri Duval

When Doucette saw the letter, she said,
"No more snooping around in strange people's houses for you—
that's finished forever!
You are the smartest mouse in the world!"

Paul and Paulette,
Claude and Claudette,
and Georges and Georgette
climbed up on his chair and hugged him.
"We are so proud!
Our beloved *Papa* is now a respectable business-mouse!"

The next day Anatole invited Gaston to be his helper.

The older mouse made a very deep bow.
"Gladly will I join you!"

Then he kissed his friend on both cheeks, and cried:
"VIVE ANATOLE! Was he content
to sit back and do *nothing* about our way of life?
NON! NON!
He is a mouse of action—a mouse of honor—
A MOUSE MAGNIFIQUE!"

And so it came to pass.

Anatole and his partner worked at the factory,
side by side in perfect harmony.

The secret stayed a secret, always.

So if you should ever meet a mouse looking for leftovers,
you will know at once
that it cannot possibly be Anatole,
the happiest, most contented mouse
in all France.